the VERY WORST ever

PiZZA PARTY POOPER

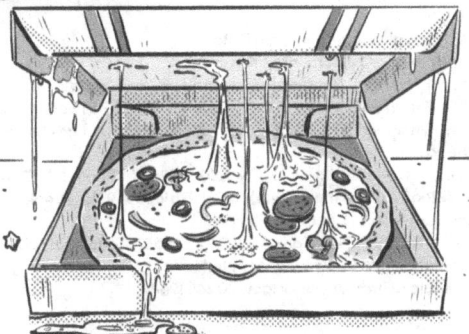

BY ANDY NONAMUS
ILLUSTRATED BY AMY JINDRA

LITTLE SIMON
NEW YORK LONDON TORONTO SYDNEY NEW DELHI

LITTLE SIMON

An imprint of Simon & Schuster Children's Publishing Division

1230 Avenue of the Americas, New York, New York 10020

First Little Simon hardcover edition September 2024

Copyright © 2024 by Simon & Schuster, LLC

Also available in a Little Simon paperback edition.

All rights reserved, including the right of reproduction in whole or in part in any form.

LITTLE SIMON is a registered trademark of Simon & Schuster, LLC, and associated colophon is a trademark of Simon & Schuster, LLC.

Simon & Schuster: Celebrating 100 Years of Publishing in 2024

For information about special discounts for bulk purchases, please contact Simon & Schuster Special Sales at 1-866-506-1949 or business@simonandschuster.com.

The Simon & Schuster Speakers Bureau can bring authors to your live event. For more information or to book an event contact the Simon & Schuster Speakers Bureau at 1-866-248-3049 or visit our website at www.simonspeakers.com.

Text by Matthew J. Gilbert

Designed by Hannah Frece

The text of this book was set in Causten Round.

Manufactured in the United States of America 0824 LAK

10 9 8 7 6 5 4 3 2 1

Library of Congress Cataloging-in-Publication Data

Names: Nonamus, Andy, author. | Jindra, Amy, illustrator.

Title: Pizza party pooper / by Andy Nonamus ; illustrated by Amy Jindra.

Description: First Little Simon edition. | New York : Little Simon, 2024. | Series: The very worst ever ; book 5 | Summary: An unlucky kid, who wishes to remain anonymous, finds himself in a competition for the Student of the Month.

Identifiers: LCCN 2024019646 (print) | LCCN 2024019647 (ebook) | ISBN 9781665959490 (paperback) | ISBN 9781665959506 (hardcover) | ISBN 9781665959513 (ebook)

Subjects: CYAC: Schools—Fiction. | Contests—Fiction.

Classification: LCC PZ7.1.N6378 Pi 2024 (print) | LCC PZ7.1.N6378 (ebook) | DDC [Fic]—dc23

LC record available at https://lccn.loc.gov/2024019646

LC ebook record available at https://lccn.loc.gov/2024019647

CONTENTS

Hey, Reader!

Thanks for checking out my story. Though I gotta warn you, I can't ever let you know my real name or what I look like. This may seem weird, but trust me, it's very important that I stay a secret.

Why? To protect myself! Seriously, these stories are super embarrassing!

Plus, you might even know me already! I could be in your class, on your baseball team, in your ballet class, or playing the tuba in your school band . . . anywhere!

Hi!

For all you know I could be sitting next to you right now!

So I went ahead and scratched out my name and put a sticker on my face, so you don't have to. You're welcome.

Now, we can both enjoy reading all about my awkward life . . . if you're into that kind of thing.

Peace out!

WHAT'S A WARTSOFF?

Something strange was happening at school.

Well, stranger than usual. See, this school wasn't like any other.

Here, the bells didn't ring. They mooed like cows.

The lockers didn't just hold books. They were doors into secret tunnels.

Oh, and the teachers didn't just dress up for work. They dressed up for fun. I'm talking wacky sunglasses and hats that played music.

Why? That was just the way!

But today, teachers wore boring clothes and the morning bell rang normally.

RIIIIING!

"That sounds awfully normal," I said, scratching my chin. "What's going on today?"

"It's the power of Wartsoff," Regina du Lar said, appearing at my side.

If you don't know, Regina is one of my best friends. Her family owns the Du Lar Video Game Emporium, so they're super rich.
(Not to mention
super cool.)

"A wart-off?" I asked, imagining gross warts.

"*Wartsoff*," a gloomy voice added at my other side. "It's someone's last name. A name more powerful than even mine."

It was my friend Glinda Alegre.

You could find her haunting the hallways or keeping guard of the secret school tunnels.

I shrugged. "I've never heard of this person."

Regina frowned. "Wartsoff's a kid in *your* class, █████████. She's throwing the entire school an all-day pizza party to celebrate her family's new pizza shop."

SCHOOL-WIDE PIZZA PARTY!

PIZZA PARTY TODAY!

THANK YOU FOR THE PIZZA KARLA WARTSOFF!

"That's why everyone's wearing boring clothes," Glinda explained. "For all the pizza stains to come."

A pizza party? All day long? Now, that *was* a pretty big deal!

I hurried to classroom 312, where I found my classmates crowded around a table with at least twelve pizza boxes.

"There you are, bro!" Jake Gold, my sportiest friend, pulled me into the crowd.

"I would've been here sooner if I'd known this was waiting!" I said, staring at the pizza boxes with starry eyes.

"Even if this is from someone named Warts–"

"Are you making fun of my last name?" a kid interrupted me.

I turned around. There stood a girl with two perfect braids, a unicorn shirt, and a frown.

(No warts, though.)

"No, no!" I said. "Warts are, uh . . . so cool!"

The girl then looked suspicious. "Do you even know my first name, ██████████?"

Okay, I felt pretty bad that she knew my name but I couldn't remember hers.

So I thought really hard.

As I dug through classroom memories, the girl's face slowly appeared in my brain. In one memory, she was telling me to stop doodling on my homework. In another, she was smacking her forehead as I bumped into the trash can.

I snapped my fingers. "Oh! You're the girl who's always telling us what to do. Kaleigh!"

She crossed her arms. "Nope. Kaleigh's not my name."

My fingers drooped. "Casey?"

Everyone around me shook their heads.

I tried again. "Camila? Katrina?"

"It's Karla!" the girl huffed. "Karla Wartsoff!"

2

POOPER ALERT!

So *this* was Wartsoff.

Yeah, I know what you're thinking. Shouldn't I know who she was by now?

The thing is, I was always busy trying to escape total disaster. During recess, I avoided the bees who liked to play tag.

And every time the water fountain flooded, we swam down the halls.

I don't even want to think about the mysterious black hole that suddenly appeared near my desk.

(It was a good thing Mr. Hughes had stuffed it with pillows. I fell into it a lot.)

So, yeah. Being me was a lot of work. Still, I wanted to make things right.

Sticking out my hand, I said, "I promise to remember your name, Karina!"

Around me, everyone groaned.

"Dude," Jake whispered. "Her name's Karla. If you forget it again, just look at the wall over there."

I followed his gaze and saw a giant wall of Karla posters. She smiled wide in each of them. They all labeled her as our Student of the Month.

When had those posters gotten there? And since when did we have a Student of the Month?!

"Oh, forget it," Karla sighed, turning to the pizza table. "Everyone's waiting for pizza, and my family stayed up all night making enough slices to last us through the all-day party. Do you want to help me pass them out?"

"Sure!" I said. "Happy to help!"

How hard could this be? Grabbing a paper plate from the table, I opened the first pizza box.

And guess what? The moment I smelled the delicious pizza, I drooled.

ALL . . . OVER . . . THE SLICES.

"Gross!" Karla cried out.

I slurped my saliva back in and laughed awkwardly. "Oopsies. I'll just clean that."

Here's a little lesson for you. Do not use a napkin to wipe pizza clean. Because a glob of cheese will get stuck on it. And when you pull the napkin back, the cheese will run down your sleeves. It will even drip on the floor, all over your shoes.

What kind of cheese was this?!

"You're ruining all the cheesy goodness!" someone cried.

"WE NEED PIZZA!" another kid shouted.

"Coming right up!" I said, panicking.

But when I reached for another slice, things got even worse. I slipped on the floor cheese and flew right into the pizza table. "GAH!" I shouted.

When I crashed into the table, the pizza boxes flew into the air. Then, they all opened over our heads. Slippery cheese, pepperoni, veggies, and slimy little fish fell out in heaps.

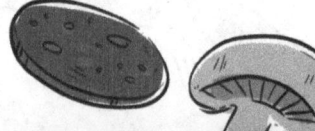

"It's raining pizza!" Jake shouted. "Open wide!"

But no one would be eating pizza. Instead, we were all covered in goop. The desks, Karla's posters, and just about everything else in the room, too.

Mr. Hughes walked in just then. "Good morning, class! Oh, goodness. What do we have here?"

"We've got a Pizza Party Pooper!" Karla cried out.

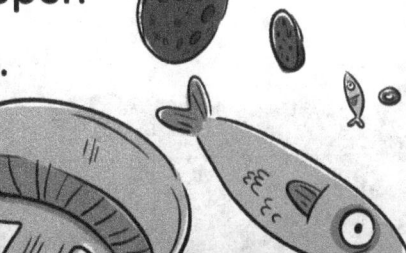

3

KARLA FACTS!

Being known as the Pizza Party Pooper was not fun. I hadn't meant to ruin anything.

I wasn't happy about it.

Class 312 wasn't happy about it.

Karla was really, really not happy about it.

"This place is a mess!" she said.

Karla looked at the pizza spill with a frown. "Now, the all-day party is totally ruined!"

Jake swiped a pepperoni from my face and ate it. "Mmm! It still tastes good."

Mr. Hughes came to the rescue quickly. "Fear not! I'll get this place cleaned up in a jiffy."

He pressed a button by the light switch. The ceiling sprinklers squeaked on and drenched us with water.

"How is this any better?" I asked.

"Just you wait . . . ," Mr. Hughes said.

He pressed the button again. This time, the ceiling shifted and became a giant fan.

WHIIIIIIIR!

Within seconds, everything was squeaky clean. A giant drain on the ground flushed the mess away.

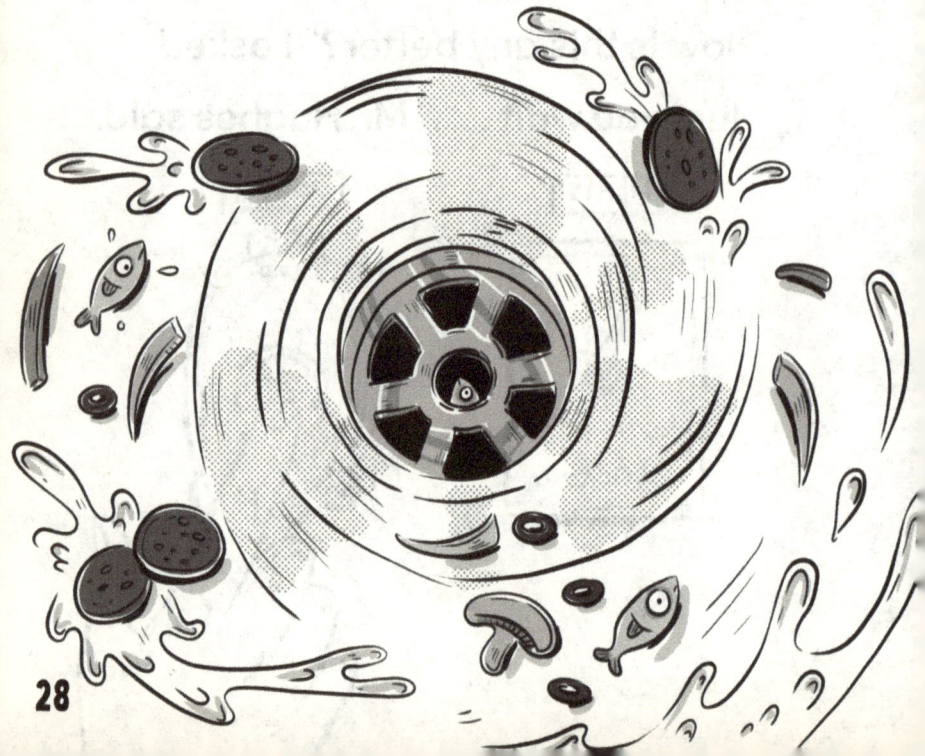

Remember how I said this school was weird? If only it had something to help clear up my guilt.

⚡

As the day went on, I learned a few things about Karla.

KARLA FACT #1

Karla knows!

If you didn't know the answer to something, Karla helped out. Even if you didn't ask for help. When it was my turn to answer a math question on the board, she stepped in and answered it for me.

$8+8=16$

"You're taking a little too long to answer, so I'm thinking you need help. Eight plus eight is sixteen," Karla said. "If you need help, just ask me. Karla knows."

The class clapped for her.

KARLA FACT #2

She did ALL the classroom chores.

Seriously. She didn't even want anyone's help, either.

Karla helped grade worksheets and she passed them out.

When the board had to be erased, she had a device that held ten erasers at once!

And when Mr. Hughes tripped into the hole in the back of homeroom, Karla lassoed him back up easily. She even closed the hole up with caution tape.

KARLA FACT #3

I didn't think she liked me very much.

Karla was so good at being helpful, it seemed like everyone waited on her to do it all.

During quiet reading time, she flipped pages for others and fluffed their beanbags. Karla did all this while reading her own book.

FLIP!

FLUFF!

From my beanbag, I asked, "Do you need any help?"

Karla shook her head without looking at me. "No, thanks. I know how to do the things the right way. Oh, your book is upside down."

I huffed. "No, it's not!"

But when I looked down, I realized she was right. I quickly flipped it over.

4

A MORNING OF BESTS

The next day, I decided to start over with my classmates. This Pizza Party Pooper name had to go!

So I kicked off my day with a morning of my bests.

When I brushed my teeth, I used my best toothpaste.

My hair was fluffier than ever.

Even my shoelaces were tied into the best bows.

The moment I arrived in class, I made sure to give everyone the best high fives.

"Good morning!" I said, giving my best smile. "Everyone sure is looking their best."

"You're looking cheery, ███████," Mr. Hughes said.

"Of course I am!" I replied. "Why wouldn't I be on this fine day?"

A kid with a green shirt glared at me. "Um, maybe it's because you pooped all over the pizza party yesterday."

I turned red. "I didn't poop!"

Karla walked into class at that moment. "We shouldn't make fun of ▇▇▇▇▇▇▇," she said. "It's not his fault he's clumsy and couldn't help out yesterday."

Clumsy?! I wasn't clumsy! I was . . .

... okay, maybe I was a little clumsy. But that didn't mean I couldn't help out. How could I prove this to Karla?

At that moment, I noticed she was holding on to a crumpled piece of paper.

"Allow me to help you throw this away!" I said, taking the ball from her hand. "Could a clumsy person do this?"

Standing on my tiptoes, I squinted my eyes and tossed the paper ball toward the trash can.

It didn't go in, though. It bounced off
the edge and rolled back to us.

Karla scooped it from the ground.
"No littering allowed in class. I'd like to
avoid any more messes."

Luckily, Mr. Hughes called the class to attention. "It's time to start the day, class! As you all know, today is Library-Gym day. We'll be heading there now to return our books."

Oh no—I'd forgotten about Library-Gym day!

Everyone else was pulling books from their backpacks.

Mr. Hughes nodded. "Looks like everyone's ready. Who will be our line leader today?"

ME! ME! ME!

I didn't have any books, but I could still make this a morning of bests by being the best line leader. Quickly, I raised my hand.

But Karla was already standing by the door. "The Student of the Month should lead the way," she said. "But you can be the caboose. That's the back of the line."

5

CHOO CHOO, CABOOSE!

Being the caboose meant you were all the way in the back of the line.

And behind everyone isn't great because you can't see much. Plus, you're doomed if anyone farts.

Jake was walking in front of me, and I knew he'd eaten a can of beans for breakfast.

(No, not the jelly kind.)

As Karla led us smoothly toward the Library-Gym, another class passed by ours. At the front was Mrs. Lee. She was a tall lady with giant glasses.

"What a fabulous line!" she said. "You have a great line leader, Mr. Hughes."

Karla bowed perfectly. "I do my best."

"So do I!" I said, waving. "I didn't choo-choo-choose to be the caboose, but I do my best to keep this train rolling for our leader up front! Can I get a 'Choo choo'?"

No one choo-chooed with me.

"Cabooses are supposed to be silent!" Karla called out. "No talking in line. It's distracting."

"Dude!" Jake whispered. "You don't have to be a Classroom Line Pooper, too."

So I just kept the train hush-hush all the way to the station. And by station, I mean the Library-Gym.

If you're familiar with that place, then you know it's not very quiet at all. The moment we got there, we had to avoid flying dodgeballs. It was easier to just crawl all the way to Mr. Bookman's desk. That's where we were supposed to drop off our books.

Mr. Bookman sat behind his desk. He looked like the gym teacher, but he was actually a librarian. "Welcome in, Mr. Hughes's class," he said. "If you'll please place your books on the return cart. After that, feel free to look around for something new to read."

I was about to go looking for comics, until I noticed Karla staying back. She tapped the side of a cart stacked with everyone's returns.

"I'll help put these books away," Karla said. "Helping out is the best part of my day."

"You're too kind." Mr. Bookman said. "I wish someone else would help you out!"

Bingo!

I'd just found another way to prove I was helpful to Karla.

Zooming over, I found another library cart with books. "I'll help out! This is my jam! It's what I'm all about! I love, uh, putting books on shelves! The dustier the better!"

"Hey, hey! That's what I like to hear," Mr. Bookman said. "Why don't we make this a little contest? Whoever puts their books back the quickest will get a gold star."

Mr. Bookman pulled out a sticker sheet with shiny gold stars. Karla's eyes widened.

"Oh, it's so on," she said.

6

SHH! NO RUNNING!

We took off running.

Well, Karla did.

I couldn't move my library cart even a little bit. I pushed and pushed, but it wouldn't budge.

"Ugh!" I groaned. "This thing isn't working."

Mr. Bookman nudged it.

"Ah!" he said. "It's because the wheels have the brakes on. Let me help you out."

The second he flipped off the wheels' brakes, the library cart took off rolling. I was holding on to it, which meant I went flying.

"AHHH!" I shouted, holding on tightly. "Watch out! Incoming cart!"

Kids jumped out of the way as I soared through the Library-Gym.

In each aisle, students were either flipping through pages or dribbling a ball. Sometimes, they did both!

There was a kickball tournament happening in the chapter book aisle.

There was a dodgeball game in the comic book section.

And a basketball game was happening in the corner with picture books.

That's where I needed to stop first. I forced the cart to make a turn toward the basketball game. As the cart turned, I grabbed a few books and tossed them into the hoop.

They flew in at the same time as the ball did.

"EXTRA POINTS!" Coach Olympia, the gym coach, shouted.

"Woo!" a player said. "Thanks, ██████!"

"No problem!" I replied, already making my way to my next stop on my speeding cart.

Next up was the board book section. That's where a soccer match was happening. Unlike at the basketball game, I couldn't find a way to zoom through. The bookshelf I needed was behind the net.

Hopping into their match, I did what any library kid should. I shushed them.

"SHHH!" I hissed. "No running in the Library-Gym!"

"Wait, what?" The players paused, confused.

Before they started moving again, I quickly tossed the books onto their shelves and went on my way.

Bit by bit, I returned the rest of the books. When I finished, I crashed into Mr. Bookman's desk.

"I...did...it," I wheezed. "I...helped... K-Karla!"

Mr. Bookman stood and clapped.

WHEEEEEZE!

"Fantastic job—you were really flying out there! Here is your prize."

Wait. My prize?

I watched as Mr. Bookman peeled a gold star sticker and handed it to me.

"I'm here! All done!" Karla said, rushing from around the corner. "I won—huh?"

"Looks like ██████████ was a little faster this time." Mr. Bookman patted my back. "You've got some competition, Karla!"

Karla did not like this. I didn't either.

She glared at me, turned around, and stomped away.

This little gold star hadn't helped at all!

7

A VERY BIG
ANNOUNCEMENT

The next day, things got even worse.

It started off normally. I was doing what every kid wanted to do . . .

. . . scraping gum from the bottoms of desks.

Yep. I was working through a big, yellow glob that smelled a little bit like banana sorbet.

(Was this where Jake was getting his gum to share?!)

Karla was also there. She was writing today's special vocabulary word on the board.

She wrote:

IRONY: THIS IS WHEN SOMETHING UNEXPECTED HAPPENS.

"I can do that for you," I offered, trying to escape the gum.

"No, thanks," Karla said. "I can do this myself."

I went back to my gum scraping glumly.

Soon, the rest of the class trickled in and found their seats.

Mr. Hughes began class a little earlier than usual. "All right, everyone, let's get the day started! I've got a very big announcement."

Wondering what it could be, we all quieted down quickly.

Mysteriously, Mr. Hughes said, "It's time to announce . . ."

He clapped his hands together and the room went dark.

". . . the new Student of the Month!" he finished.

With another clap, the lights came back on.

Mr. Hughes was suddenly wearing a cape and a bow tie. He looked like he was at an awards show.

A large red curtain now covered the wall where all Karla's Student of the Month posters were hung. Oh, and did I mention the microphone that plopped down from the ceiling?

(Just how many things were hiding up there?)

The class whispered excitedly. I could barely hold still. I'd helped Karla out so much that she was sure to win again. Maybe she would forgive me for all the chaos I'd caused!

At her desk, Karla lined up her pencils perfectly.

Mr. Hughes spoke into the microphone. "Students, beanbag chairs, and overwatered cactus. This month's Student of the Month is . . ."

A drumroll played . . .

. . . everyone leaned in . . .

. . . and the strangest thing ever happened.

Mr. Hughes swept the curtain to the side. It revealed a poster of Karla, but she looked a bit funny. She had a red hoodie on instead of her unicorn shirt. Oh, and her hair wasn't black. It was just a messy glob.

Wait a minute. That wasn't Karla.

That was . . . ME!

"Congratulations, ▓▓▓▓▓▓▓ !" Mr. Hughes said. "You are Student of the Month!"

STUDENT OF THE MONTH

8

LOOK! ANOTHER ANNOUNCEMENT!

Wait. What? Huh? What just happened?!

My eyes darted everywhere to make sure everyone else had heard the same thing.

"M-me?" I said. "I'm ... Student ... of ... the Month?"

"That's right!" Mr. Hughes said.

He pulled on a lever and confetti poured down.

And you know what? It felt amazing!

"WOW!" I shouted, leaping up and down. "This is . . . this is . . . WOW!"

Jake rolled around in the confetti, throwing it up in the air. "You go, bro! You're number one!"

I took the microphone from Mr. Hughes and faced the class. "Thank you all so much! I would like to thank the cactus in the corner for always needing water. And you all, for dropping all sorts of things that need cleaning up. Oh, and myself! Because I did all the things! I, ██████████, promise to be the Best Student of the Month of all time."

I took a bow, expecting to hear my classmates clapping. But except for Jake's cheering, it was completely silent.

Mr. Hughes chuckled. "I wasn't quite done yet."

My eyes widened as I stared at the ground. He wasn't done? What did that mean?

"The thing is . . . ," Mr. Hughes said, "you're not the only Student of the Month."

He then swept the curtain again, revealing a second poster next to mine.

"Your second Student of the Month is . . . KARLA WARTSOFF!" Mr. Hughes announced.

STUDENT OF THE MONTH

STUDENT OF THE MONTH (ALSO!)

Now, everyone burst into applause. Even the cactus in the corner!

Where Karla stood, confetti also rained on her. But she didn't look as excited as I'd felt. Instead, she was glaring at me.

"That's never happened before!" I heard someone say over the cheering.

"I can't believe ██████████ and Karla are sharing the spot!" someone else said.

Jake backflipped over to Karla and threw confetti on her, too. "You go, girl! You're also number one! Wooo! Two number ones! That's so confusing!"

Mr. Hughes placed a golden medallion around each of our necks. "Congratulations, both of you! To celebrate, we'll have a pizza party redo on Friday. Why don't you guys work together on planning something fun?"

"Okay!" I said. "What do you say, Karla? Ready to work together?"

But Karla was still glaring at me.

I smiled awkwardly.

This was going to be a very long month.

9

A SOUP-RISE MEETING

When you're Student of the Month, you notice everything.

When I passed out papers, I learned everyone's names and also just how much they doodled on their work.

I even found out which kid was wiping his boogers on the reading wall.

(That's right . . . his boogers!)

But the most important thing I learned was that Karla spent the rest of the day being quiet. That afternoon, she barely fluffed the reading beanbags. She didn't notice how much the eraser shavings had piled up on the ground.

When the lunch bell mooed, I made up my mind to go talk to her.

Because our cafeteria was also the playground, I hopscotched my way through the lunch tables to find Karla. She was sipping soup all alone....

... on top of the jungle gym.

"Oh, great," I grumbled. I hopped and grabbed the monkey bars. It was time to make things right, one swing at a time.

"I...need to...exercise more," I said, wheezing as I climbed up next to her. "H-hi, Karla!"

Karla didn't even look at me.

Awkwardly, I reached down for the sandwich in my pocket. But it wasn't there.

I threw my head back. "Aw, man! I think all that hopscotch made me drop my lunch."

She reached into her lunch box and handed me a small, warm container.

"What's this?" I asked.

"I always bring an extra soup," Karla said. "In case anyone forgets lunch."

"Of course you do." I smiled. "That's why you're the best Student of the Month ever!"

"Not anymore," she grumbled. "You're everyone's favorite Student of the Month now. You even got Mr. Bookman's gold star. And no one minds that you ruined my pizza party anymore."

"I am really sorry about that," I said. "I didn't mean to make a mess of everything. I'm just a little unlucky sometimes. But I've been trying to make it up to you by helping out!"

Karla looked unsure. "You were just

trying to help me? I thought you were trying to take my spot as everyone's helper."

I shook my head. "No, no! You've totally got this."

"Even though I'm always telling everyone what to do?" Karla asked.

Oh boy. I did feel pretty bad for saying that. "I was wrong. You're really helpful, and that's why everyone wants you to be Student of the Month every time. No one keeps everything in line like you do!"

Karla smiled at this. "Thanks, ███████ And ... I'm sorry for being so rude to you the past couple days. I think it's very nice that you stepped up to help me."

I smiled. "How about we start planning this pizza party redo for Friday? We can mix our brains together and really do something special for everyone! No more Pizza

CLINK!

Party Poopers. Instead, we'll be Pizza Party Partners."

Karla said, "Deal!"

We clanged our soup containers together.

10

PIZZA PARTY PARTNERS

Even though Karla and I were total opposites, we actually made a great pair.

We went together like chocolate sauce on a hot dog! Or like berry jam on spaghetti!

You might think those things don't go together, but you'd be surprised.

Mr. Hughes, Karla, and I got to class early to set up on Friday.

"We have the right amount of healthy and sugary snacks, music, and a few games thanks to Regina du Lar," Karla said, checking things off a list. "Are you ready to let the class in, fellow Student of the Month?"

I gave her a thumbs-up. "I sure am, fellow Student of the Month!"

"Let's do this!" Mr. Hughes cheered. He opened the classroom door.

Outside, all our classmates were eagerly waiting to be let in.

"Welcome to PIZZA PALOOZA!" Karla and I shouted, throwing our hands up.

"Whoa!" the kids all said, their eyes big and shiny.

Karla zoomed to the left side of the room. "Over here, you can play classroom games and do fun brain teasers. It's important to learn!"

"And over here," I said, pointing to the right, "we have finger painting, mini piñatas, and charades! It's important to have fun!"

"Hold on," a girl said. "Where's the pizza? Did ▉▉▉▉▉ drop it again?"

"Not this time," Karla said, laughing.

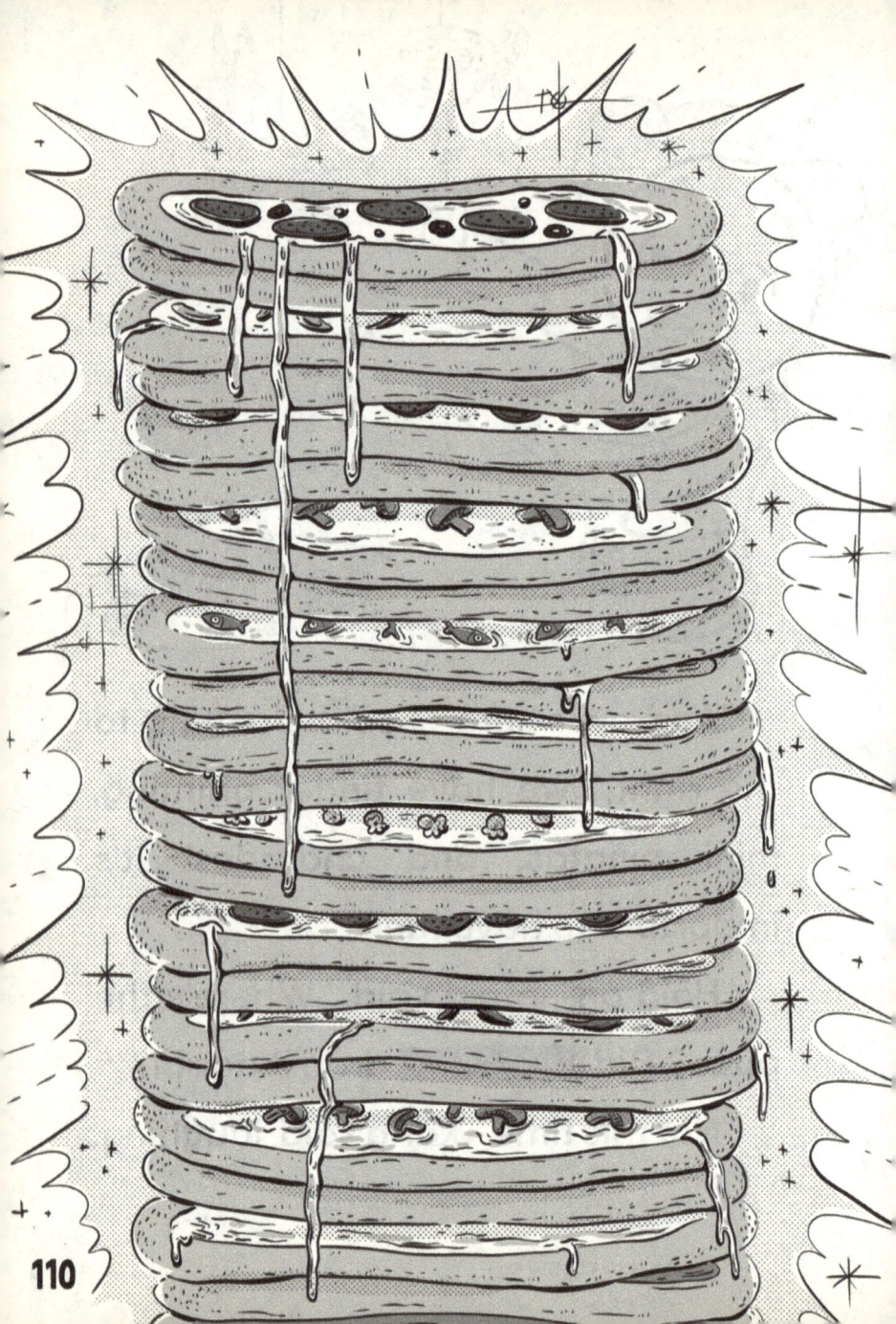

"Just look right over here."

On the long table where I'd ruined the pizza last week sat a tall item covered by a box. It was so tall, it nearly reached the ceiling.

"Fellow students," I said. "Thanks to Karla's parents' amazing new pizza shop, we don't just have a regular ol' pizza pie."

"It's a pizza tower!" Karla shouted.

She popped the top of the box off and revealed the most incredible stack of pizzas. It was almost like a cake.

"WHOAAAA!" everyone shouted.

"Maybe you should do the serving this time," I said to Karla.

"Okay!" she said.

Then, something very strange happened.

When Karla reached for a slice with the pizza server, the pizza tower started leaning over. And before we could do anything about it, the tower began to fall.

"NOOOOOOOO!" I shouted.

But it was no use.

The pizzas fell, cheese goo flew onto everything, and the entire class was once again covered in delicious food.

We all stared at Karla in silence.

But then Karla burst into laughter. "What's a party without a little mess?"

"I say we eat this mess up!" Jake shouted.

So that's what we ended up doing. It made me feel very lucky to have such amazing friends in my class. (Especially the messy ones.)

HERE'S A PEEK AT ████████ 'S NEXT ADVENTURE!

Imagine the scariest place ever.

Is it a gloomy vampire's castle? Or maybe a shark-infested volcano? Or worse yet . . . a vampire's castle inside a shark-infested volcano?!

Pffft! I was in an even worse place.

Here, it smelled like moldy sneakers.

An excerpt from *Go for the Gold*

Kids charged at you from all corners. Books fell from shelves and tripped you. I'm talking about . . .

. . . *the Library-Gym.*

(Yeah, you read that right. It's the library and the gym.)

My class was in the last round of scooter soccer practice. It's as wacky as it sounds. You hop on a scooter, wheel around, and kick the ball into the right net.

While they played, I hid behind a library cart. I wasn't alone, though. I'd met two new friends—Shiny Penny and Dust Bunny.

An excerpt from *Go for the Gold*

"Don't judge me for not playing," I whispered. "Remember that time I threw a boomerang right into the light bulb?"

The Library-Gym didn't have working lights for weeks.

FWEEET! I jumped at the sound of Coach Olympia's whistle.

Peeking from behind the cart, I saw her standing on one of the library tables. She might *look* sweet, but Coach Olympia didn't mess around.

"You call that scootin'?" she shouted. "That won't win the after-school scooter soccer tournament!

An excerpt from *Go for the Gold*

Look at Jake Gold—*he's* got what it takes."

Jake swooshed past me, did a cool backflip on his scooter, and kicked the ball into the net. He was one of my best friends and one of the best kids in gym. His parents were star athletes, after all.

"SCORE!" his team cheered.

"Go, Jake!" I whisper-cheered.

They were doing just fine without me. But then something terrible happened.

Jake looked *right* at me. "What are you doing back there?" he asked.

An excerpt from *Go for the Gold*

"The game is over here, silly!"

Everyone turned to look at me. Coach Olympia did *not* look happy.

"Get back in the game, ▮▮▮▮▮▮▮!" she shouted. "No cheating!"

"I wasn't cheating at scooter soccer," I squealed. "I was just *hiding* from it."

"No excuses!" she shouted. "You just cost your team two points."

DING! The scoreboard subtracted two points from my team.

"Dude!" a kid complained. "How could you?"

"So long, Shiny Penny," I said.

An excerpt from *Go for the Gold*